This book belongs to

....

For my daughter,
my small, precious hatchling;
for my Leigh, who sees me

The Heartsong of Wonder Quinn

Kate Gordon

UQP

1
First day

Wonder Quinn sat on the roof of Direleafe Hall. There was a flickering in her belly. A tickling. Like moths, beating their wings at her insides.

Hollowbeak noticed, of course. Hollowbeak noticed everything about Wonder, even a flickering deep inside her. He shook his small, dark head and sighed.

Every year.

Down below them, girls tumbled through the high iron gates that separated the school from all of the world. The gates were as old and life-worn as the hall itself, but the children were new and clean and shining.

From where Wonder and Hollowbeak sat, it was tricky to see who was who. The students dressed in identical uniforms: navy pinafores that fell down to their calves, paler blue cardigans on top of those and blue socks held up by garters.

Some of the girls grumbled about the uniforms. They called them old-fashioned and dowdy. Wonder didn't see it like that. She liked her uniform. It made her feel like she belonged. She belonged to this old, dusty school, and she belonged to the girls, even if they might not know it.

She searched the bobbing heads and shiny faces. That one – was that Amelia?

And was that one Eloise? And that one ...

She knew that head – that snow-white hair. She knew that upturned nose and those cheekbones, sharp as arrowheads.

Georgiana Kinch.

She tamped down a shudder so Hollowbeak would not see, looked away from the pale-haired girl and recommenced her game of memory.

She knew Alice from her pale pink bow and Jemima from her tight black ringlets.

But, of course, some of them she wouldn't know. There would be newlings, naturally, in first form.

And there might – the flickering thing in Wonder's belly began to quicken – there might even be a new girl in her class. Someone from across the seas, perhaps? Someone who had seen things.

Someone who knew things. Someone who had walked off the edge of one map and on to another.

Wonder had always wanted to travel through the skies and over the wide, wild lands and across the seas. She had dreamed of bathing in waterfalls and running with untamed horses and eating a ripe pink mango.

But she was stuck here at Direleafe Hall and so ... a friend from far-off lands might be the next best thing.

But, of course, it didn't matter – not really, not at all – where the new girl might be from. As long as she liked Wonder. As long as she *saw* her.

A friend.

Now, that would be a thing.

A friend who saw her heart and loved it and knew it was good.

It was a thing that Wonder had hoped for, each of these years at Direleafe. It hadn't happened yet. But this year – Wonder grasped onto the charcoal shingles even more tightly – this year it just might.

Last night, like every year on the night before first day, Wonder could not find sleep. She'd tossed and turned in her little nook, which was at the back of the school archives in the attic.

The archive room was newer than all the other rooms of Direleafe Hall, but it was still old. And nobody visited it any more because it contained only the most ancient of cabinets, which held only the dustiest of files and the oldest of stories.

The newer cabinets and the newer files lived down in Ms Gallow's office. But the old attic archives that Wonder called home was a place for only dead, dust-covered things. Yet it was Wonder's, and she loved it and, usually, she found solace and comfort there, and a place to rest her weary head and dream all the happy things.

But not on the last night of holidays. Not ever on the last night before first day. On those nights – those edge-of-cliff eves – Wonder's eyes seemed glued open. She felt like a doll with no eyelids or a waxwork imitation of a human that would never sleep, never dream.

She might have believed it to be true – that she was wax only and not real at all – if her brain hadn't been so filled with things. Surely waxworks and dolls didn't buzz with thrumming thrills at the prospect of new years, new girls, new maybes and perchances.

Wonder had tried, last night, to think of pretty things, like peacocks and golden-mote faeries dancing in sunbeams. She'd tried to read. She'd even tried singing to herself. She sang herself a lullaby, from when she was small. One her mother used to sing her. It always (usually) put her right to sleep.

My small, precious hatchling,
In your nest, tucked in tight,
Flutter down your eyelids
And bid the stars goodnight ...

The trouble was, *always* and *usually* didn't apply on first-day eve and, instead, she found herself only missing her mother. But only for a little while. Before the thrumming thrill came back.

A new year! New students.

Maybe a friend.

Now, that would be a thing.

A friend who saw her heart. A friend who saw her. *A friend to wind up the clockwork key and begin her again. Make her new.*

How could a child sleep when the possibility of something new was waiting just around the corner?

Now, on the roof, Wonder rubbed at her eyes and yawned. Her whole body felt worn and weary. But her mind was bubbling like ginger beer. She shuffled a little down the charcoal shingles. A tiny bit closer, so she might see the girls a tiny bit more clearly.

She could see more faces now – Genevieve, Evangeline, Lily – all of the girls who had stared blankly through her every previous year, as if she were part of the furniture. But she didn't feel badly towards them. They simply weren't *meant* to be her friends.

One day, one year, she would find her perfect person. The one whose soul was the perfect mirror of hers. The one who knew her, who she was, entirely, and saw that she was good. The one who saw that she was golden inside.

Not grey.

And then, when she found her person, none of it would matter. Not losing her mother. Not living in the back of the school archives, invisible and alone. Not even having, for her only companion, a temperamental crow called Hollowbeak.

He shook his feathers and looked up at her with those black-button eyes that seemed to see every inch of Wonder's soul. *You're thinking it again, aren't you*? he said. *You're thinking that this will be 'the year'*. He gave a little noise that sounded like a snort.

'Don't hex me, Hollowbeak,' Wonder growled. 'You just want me all to yourself.'

Now, why would I want that? You can't even fly. I don't need you. A crow needs only himself, entirely. But you need me.

'Why, exactly?' Wonder asked, but she knew in her deepest self that it was true. Hollowbeak had been there ever since her mother died. He looked after her. He provided for her. He was the best friend she'd ever had. Even as he professed to need only himself, he was at her side the moment she called. Just as her mother had always been. And just like her mother, he told her how to live, how to *exist*. He gave her form and shape and he helped her to survive in this strange, confusing motherless world.

But he was wrong about one thing – he wasn't *all* she needed.

When her mother was here with her, curled around her, dancing her through life, she never felt lonely. But now she felt an aching within her. A hole that Hollowbeak could not fill.

She leaned her chin on her palm and watched as the last of the girls trickled inside Direleafe Hall. Their feet left furrows on the dew-wet grass and black daubs on the grey stone steps. They moved in through the arched wooden doors, the hinges browned and groaning with age. And then they were swallowed up by the door, by the grey brick walls, by the stones. They were a school of blue-and-grey-scaled fish, made shining by the sea, swimming into the mouth of a whale.

All except for one of them.

That last one.

That last one – a straggler – was new.

She was tiny, thin, with a blaze of red hair. She carried an enormous backpack that threatened to tip her over. She huffed and puffed to keep up with the other girls.

Then, she stopped, panting with exertion.

And she looked up to the sky.

Right at Wonder.

2 Ms Gallow's classroom

Wonder Quinn sat in her usual seat, at the back of Ms Gallow's classroom.

The classroom was old and it was dusty and it was so wintry-cold, due to the ancient, wind-leaking windows, that the girls wore woollen gloves so their fingers could move enough to write.

The desks had been in their same soldier rows for a hundred years and more besides. Their hinges creaked and there were cracks in the wood and, on Wonder's desk, there was a knot that looked like a badger's head. It had watched her, knowingly, for all these years. For this had been Wonder's seat every year and every year the seat beside it had stayed empty, and the badger looked at her and the empty chair and it judged them both.

And perhaps that was *why* the seat beside her was always empty: nobody wants to sit next to a judgemental badger.

Wonder watched, each first day of school, as the new girls peered at the empty chair, as their faces took on a funny expression, as they gave a little shudder and pulled their cardigans closer, as they moved quickly away to another seat.

Wonder tried her best to ignore it and have hope that one year, on the right year, the *right girl* would take the seat.

And this year, she did.

The girl with the red hair didn't frown, didn't shiver, and she sat down beside Wonder without even looking – at the desk or at her new neighbour. She flopped into the chair, threw her bag underneath it and huffed, 'Well, that was a trial.'

She put her pencil case and workbook on the table and ran her hands over the bumpy surface. 'Hmm,' she murmured. And then she gave the desk a pat and said, 'I think you're meant to be mine.'

Then, she turned to Wonder. 'Odd little place, this, isn't it? This funny old Direleafe Hall. I'm Mabel Clattersham, by the way. Transferred here from Wolsey's. Didn't like it there and they didn't like me, and that was the end of that.'

'I'm ... I'm Wonder,' Wonder gasped. 'Wonder Quinn.' She impressed herself greatly, with the talking. She hadn't talked to another person – not *really* – for such a long time. The girls never spoke to her. The teachers never called on her.

Hollowbeak told her it was because they didn't know how. They didn't – even the teachers – know how to respond to a child whose mother was dead and who lived at the back of an office full of dull and dusty things.

He said that was part of the reason, too, why they never visited her there. Who knows how to visit a girl with so much sadness? Who knows what to say?

And then there was the fear, of course – that the grief would rub off on the visitor, as if the misery of it coated every surface.

They think they'll become you if they come too close, he told her.

So nobody visited her. Nobody looked at her.

Another reason for it, Hollowbeak explained, was because she faded.

The other girls were all exciting, in one way or another. They glowed. They had talents. They laughed loudly. They ran and jumped and squealed.

Wonder was quiet. Wonder whispered. Wonder dwindled into the background and she had no particular talents, except that she was very good at watching.

Wonder was grey. Wonder was the same as the walls and the floor.

But Mabel Clattersham saw her.

'Pleased to meet you, Wonder Quinn,' Mabel said, with a smile. 'Let's be friends, shall we?'

Friends.

Wonder sucked in a breath.

Friends!

She had said it, hadn't she?

It was real.

It was almost as if Wonder could see the word, hovering in the air in front of her.

Friends.

It was real.

Mabel was real and Wonder was real and she had said that word – that golden word.

Friends.

So. That was a thing.

3
Below the silver birch

Wonder and Mabel sat below the silver birch tree, in the shadowy part of the grounds.

It was Hollowbeak's favourite tree. He said that the twigs were just the right size for his small claws to cling to. That was part of it, certainly, but the real reason Hollowbeak loved the silver birch was because it was *strange.*

The tree, like Hollowbeak, was a bent and twisted thing, its bark as silver as twilight and its branches as black as midnight. It was peculiar and it was old and it seemed somehow imbued with age and wisdom, and Hollowbeak felt in it a kindred spirit. He loved to perch on a branch and gaze upon all below him and feel as if he were the Raven Master of all he surveyed.

He had told all of this to Wonder before, and Wonder had told him he was king of all the world and had nuzzled his soft black feathers (he had shrugged her away, of course).

On this day, though, Hollowbeak was giving Wonder the irrits. He watched her and Mabel from that spindly twig, his button eyes narrowed, his beak haughty and, when Mabel spoke, he shook his head and sometimes even snorted.

Wonder got the feeling that Hollowbeak thought Mabel was silly. Maybe that was because Mabel *was* a bit silly, Wonder thought. But in a good way.

Mabel was funny and bold and shimmery with colour. She wasn't loud, like the other girls. She didn't squeal. Her voice was like a tickling feather. But she knew so many jokes and she knew how to smile at Wonder as if she were a lovely thing. As if she were yellow or pink, instead of grey.

Golden.

Wonder thought she might like to listen to Mabel Clattersham talk forever.

Hollowbeak was wrong and he was vexing, the way he peered down like that, so pompously, and when Mabel went home later that day, Wonder meant to have strong words with him.

But for now ...

Now, she tried to ignore him and think only of her friend.

Mabel had brown bread sandwiches for lunch, with banana and honey inside. Wonder thought it would taste like sunbeams.

'Would you like some?' Mabel asked. 'I don't have much of an appetite today.'

Wonder shook her head. 'No, thank you.'

'You've not eaten anything!' Mabel protested.

Wonder lifted a shoulder and smiled. 'Tell me another joke,' she said.

Mabel looked up into the branches of the tree. Hollowbeak gave a snort and then a disgruntled caw. 'Why is a raven like a writing desk?' Mabel asked, finally.

Wonder smiled. 'I know this one. I like this one. My mother used to tell it to me and I would lie awake at night, thinking on it ...' She trailed off, remembering.

She had stayed awake, far past bedtime, snuggled in her warm bed, her mother snoring softly beside her. And she had imagined. She had imagined a raven, knocking at her bedroom window.

It wasn't a bad raven.

It was a friend.

She'd told her mother, in the morning, and her mother had held her tight and told her that it made sense. Because of what crows and ravens really are.

Wonder shook herself. Mabel was staring at her, curiously.

'Yes, it's a good riddle,' Wonder said. 'I like it a lot, even though it isn't very funny. *Should* a riddle always be funny?'

'I don't think so. Not always. Not if it's clever,' Mabel said. 'I like funny things and clever things, too. I like *all* things. Why do I have to like all things? That's too many things to like.'

'But there's a lot of time,' Wonder pointed out. 'There's *so* much time, for all the things.'

Mabel lay flat on her back. The sun, dappled between the leaves of the tree, made her into a glowing wood nymph. 'A raven and a writing desk both produce notes, though they are very flat,' Mabel murmured, answering the riddle. She smiled at Wonder, who gazed down at her in rapture.

'Where did you come from?' asked Wonder.

'The stars,' laughed Mabel. But she knew what Wonder meant. 'I came from the city, but my parents thought I'd benefit from the clean country air.'

She looked sideways into the light at Wonder. 'I care less about air,' she said, 'and more about doing *things*.'

'What sort of things?'

'All the things,' Mabel breathed. 'My parents won't let me do any of the things. I can't eat shellfish. I can't bathe in the sea. I can't go out at night. And there's no sea in the city, anyway, and there's no night either, really, because the lights are always on. In the city, you can't do any of the things that mean anything. You can't be free there.'

'Why not?' Wonder asked, enchanted.

She'd never been to the city. She'd heard, though, that there were buildings there even taller than Direleafe Hall, and grand hotels where men stood outside in tall hats and gloves, and the ladies danced in beaded gowns, long into the evening.

And you could buy any kind of food you wanted, whenever you wanted it. And there were bookshops on every corner, and libraries with twenty thousand books inside.

'Muggers, mostly,' Mabel replied, airily, and Wonder was too bashful to ask what a mugger was.

So, for a little while there was silence, except for the far-off noises of the other girls, the lizards in the grass and scoffing Hollowbeak.

Snort.

Caw.

Shush, thought Wonder, loudly, hoping that he could hear her thoughts in the way it often seemed he could.

'Where is your house?' Mabel finally asked Wonder.

Wonder supposed she knew the

question had been coming. She knew she'd have to tell Mabel, sooner or later. But inside of her, something shrank and cowered.

What if she told Mabel all of the things that were wrong and missing and broken in her life and Mabel decided, like the other girls, that she couldn't possibly understand Wonder? That she couldn't talk to her any more? That they couldn't be *friends*?

That would be ... a tragedy.

But Wonder didn't know how to lie. She'd never learned. So, she looked at her pale fingers and bravely told the truth.

'I have no house,' said Wonder. 'But I do have a room.' She met Mabel's eyes. 'Would you like to see it?'

4
Wonder's home

Wonder and Mabel sat on Wonder's rough woollen blanket at the back of the archives.

Wonder picked at a loose thread and waited, with an ever-growing knot in her belly, for Mabel to speak again. Outside the window, Hollowbeak sat on a twig of the silver birch tree, torturing an amaranthine worm. Occasionally, he'd look inside, but when Wonder looked back, he turned away.

She'll hate it, Wonder heard him gripe.

It's so dingy and dull. She'll run away down the stairs. You mark my words. She'll run away and she won't come back. And perhaps that is for the best.

'It's ... brilliant,' Mabel said.

Wonder dropped her blanket thread and looked up at Mabel, her mouth a perfect 'O'. 'Really?' she whispered. 'You like it?'

'I love it!' giggled Mabel. 'It's your own little world!'

Wonder looked around her room, imagining she saw it through Mabel's eyes. The rows of leather-bound books, blanketed in grit, seemed to take on a new kind of magic. The candle she kept in an old bottle, for when the nights grew too dark, seemed more romantic and curious.

Heroines in books had candles,

didn't they? They read by them at night-time, just as Wonder did. She had long yearned for a lantern of her very own, but now ... now, that small candle seemed just right, when seen by Mabel's eyes. Even the cobwebs seemed more silver, seemed to shine. And her rough woollen blanket ...

She'd held on to that blanket for all these many years, although she didn't really need it, because she imagined it smelled like her mother. Probably, it didn't, any more, and probably all trace of her mother – her skin cells and discarded hairs and all of that – was long, long gone, made into more of that seemingly infinite dust.

But Wonder *imagined* that the blanket still held her. That her mother was part of the blanket and the blanket was part of her. Its decrepitude hadn't mattered at all until the moment before Mabel sat down upon it, and then it had seemed the very worst blanket to ever exist.

But now ...

Now, it seemed like the very most luxurious of all bedlinens. Now, it seemed plumper and cosier, and *fancy,* even.

'It's all right up here.' She shrugged, flushing red as she played down her fizzing pride. 'It's lonely, sometimes.'

Mabel shook her head. 'It's not lonely. It's *free*. At home, my mum and dad are always hovering around me like gadflies. When school finishes today, they'll be down there, rattling the bars, desperate to see me. That's why I was late this morning. They wanted to walk me in and carry my bags. Meet the teacher.

Make sure I found the right desk…' Mabel sighed, rolling her eyes.

But then she saw something in Wonder's face – noticed some flinch or glint of sadness. 'What about you?' she said, gently. 'What about your parents? Your mum and dad? Where are they?'

'Mother,' Wonder corrected. 'I only ever had my mother. My …' She searched for the word that Mabel had used. 'My *mum*. And she left me a long time ago.'

'Oh …' Mabel inclined her head. 'You must miss her. Of course. But you're lucky in some ways, too. You can do whatever you want.'

Wonder grinned back. 'That's true.'

'Did you cry lots?' Mabel asked, softly. 'When she went away?'

Wonder hesitated. Inside, her shame felt too big for her skin. But she knew she couldn't lie. 'I didn't cry,' she admitted.

'I don't cry much, either,' Mabel said, nodding. 'Even though people say that I should.'

Mabel gave a little cough then, and she seemed to turn a bit pale, but it was dark and gloomy in Wonder's room, without the candle lit, so maybe it was only Wonder's eyes playing tricks. Wonder was the pale one, not Mabel. Mabel was made of sunshine.

Then, directly above Wonder's ceiling, the old brass school bell began its impatient clanging. Lunchbreak was over. It was time again for classes.

Mabel stood up. She held out her hand to Wonder. 'Help you up?' she said.

Wonder hesitated. She thought how nice it would be to hold Mabel's hand. It would be warm, she thought. But she shook her head. 'It's all right,' she said. 'I'm used to doing it myself.'

'You have me now,' said Mabel.

And Wonder felt so huge and glowing inside she was sure it must be visible.

But she still stood up by herself.

She'll see right through you, she heard Hollowbeak caw. *She'll leave you eventually. It's only a matter of time.*

'Enough, Hollowbeak,' hissed Wonder.

He was wrong. Mabel would not leave her. Not ever. How could a thing so perfect ever be allowed to leave?

5
Georgiana Kinch

Wonder and Mabel sat side by side, back at their desks in Ms Gallow's classroom.

Ms Gallow stood at the front of the room, writing on the blackboard. Her fingers were white with the chalk. The prints of them made smudges around the letters, and these smudges looked like small bugs, crawling.

This time – this *writing* time – was, usually, Wonder's favourite part of the lesson. She loved watching the words appear on the board – perfect white against perfect black. And the words themselves were like flowers blooming.

Today, the words were from a book that Wonder loved.

Wonder loved *all* books, of course. Books talked to her, when nobody else would. They always had. When Wonder's mother was busy teaching, she'd leave her precious girl with a stack of books for company. The characters were Wonder's first friends. And when her mother returned from lessons, Wonder would excitedly tell her all about what she and her friends had got up to, and Wonder's mother would say, 'How lucky I am, to have such capable nursemaids between those pages, to take care of my darling girl.'

Now her mother was gone, books had been her most constant companions, aside from Hollowbeak. The library was her favourite place to sit during rainy-day lunchtimes. On sunny days, she stayed outside with Hollowbeak, of course, but when it rained, she made herself very small in the very back corner of the library and read until the bell clanged. And then, after school, she went there again until it was too dark to see.

Wonder had read every book in the library at least three times. Some, she'd read over and over until she knew every word.

The book that Ms Gallow quoted from was one of those books. Wonder mouthed the words as they appeared on the blackboard:

'"Where do you go, when you're dreaming?" the boy asked the silver-eyed girl.

"I breathe out and I begin to float. I float up to the clouds and further. I float up to the stars."'

'You know this one?' asked Mabel beside her.

Wonder nodded. 'I know all of them.'

'It sounds magical,' Mabel replied, grinning.

In the chair in front of Mabel, a girl twisted around. Her hair was white as snow and held back tightly from her face with a ribbon the colour of currant jam. Her dark eyes were narrowed. Her lips were pressed together so they bleached into whiteness, just like her hair.

'You're new,' she said. 'You're weird.'

Wonder turned quickly to Mabel, her chest feeling fluttery. She wanted to warn Mabel not to speak. It was a bad idea, *always*, to speak to Georgiana Kinch.

Wonder knew this not because she had ever done it, but because she had seen other girls do it. If Georgiana didn't like you, nobody did. And Georgiana didn't like anybody who talked back to her or argued.

'I'm not weird,' Mabel replied. 'I'm nothing you say I am. I am boundless.'

Everyone in the class turned now, to stare. Even Ms Gallow placed her chalk down and looked at the girls, wiping her powdery fingers on her long, dark skirt.

'I do not abide talking in my class,' she said. Her eyes were on Mabel.

Wonder felt her skin bristling. It almost felt, because Mabel sat so close, as if Ms Gallow was looking at her.

'You are new,' Ms Gallow said, nodding at Mabel.

'I am Mabel Clattersham,' said Mabel.

There was a beat – a pause that seemed empty and yet full of *everything* – as Ms Gallow stared at Mabel and almost-Wonder.

And then she spoke. And it was made of spikes. 'You will still be punished after class,' she said. 'Even though you are Mabel Clattersham.'

And Wonder called out, because she could not stop herself, because Mabel was her *friend*, 'What about Georgiana? Ms Gallow, what about Georgiana?'

Nobody except Mabel paid her any attention. She looked at Wonder and smiled. 'Thank you for trying,' she said. 'You are a good friend. But I don't mind being in trouble.'

As Ms Gallow turned back to the board, Georgiana slowly swivelled to them again. Her eyes were steel and midwinter frost. 'Mabel Clattersham,' she hissed below her breath, 'you are a pale, sickly little turnip of a *thing* and I will roast you and cut you up and eat you alive.'

Mabel, as quick as a metronome pendulum, replied, 'You might. But you'll find a turnip can bite back. And its bite can make your belly dreadful sore.'

Georgiana went bright red, then. Her nostrils flared and her eyes narrowed, and the effect was, on the whole, reminiscent of an overripe baneberry. She said nothing more, but there was something in the silence more ominous than any possible words.

'Well. Ain't *she* a delightful miss,' Mabel murmured, rolling her eyes at Wonder.

‘She’s a snake,’ said Wonder. ‘Some people say she’s a Queen Bee, but she’s not at all. She’s a fierce albino cobra.’

‘I don’t mind snakes,’ said Mabel. ‘At least they’re obvious in their evil. She’s not a snake. She’s a kitten, hiding its claws beneath white velvet fur. Nobody sees it but us or, if they do, they pretend they don’t because they know her swipes are worse than any snake bite.’

‘That’s so true,’ murmured Wonder. Why hadn’t she seen it before? ‘When you are punished, I’ll come with you,’ she added. ‘I won’t leave you alone.’

Mabel smiled, then, and Wonder felt as if she might jump on the table and howl with the happiness of it all.

6
Punishment

Wonder and Mabel sat in the library. Ms Gallow perched behind the librarian's desk, reading a novel about haunted houses and dark nights on the moors. Mabel and Wonder wrote lines.

I will not speak out of turn, Wonder wrote, because this is what Ms Gallow had instructed. Her pencil was worn to a nub. It barely made a scratch on her paper. But she liked it. She liked making *some* mark.

Usually, in lessons, Wonder made no

mark at all on her paper because she lost her last pencil a long time ago and she was too anxious to ask for another. But Mabel had given her one of her spares and, even though it was worn down and a bit chewed and splintered, Wonder loved it.

A present from a *friend*.

That was a thing, wasn't it?

Wonder looked over at Mabel's writing. Her eyes widened. Mabel was not writing lines. She was writing ... her *own* things. Ms Gallow would not be happy.

'What are you doing?' Wonder whispered. 'Those are not the words ... That's not what Ms Gallow said.'

Mabel shrugged. 'Life's too short for lines,' she whispered. She finished her last word with a flourish that looked something like a blown-away feather, and she passed her page to Wonder.

'What ... is it?' Wonder asked, as she scanned the page. It looked a bit like a poem. She began to read it:

Life is too tiny
For lines,
For boxes,
For smallness ...

'Not that side,' said Mabel, quickly, and she snatched the paper away and flipped it onto its belly. She tapped on the words with a finger.

This side was like a poem, too, but of a different sort.

Steal something.
Leap into the sky.

Touch a star.
Make someone feel pure happiness.
Throw a pie.
Hold a baby bird.
Break someone's heart.

'Tell me what it means,' said Wonder. 'Tell me what it *is*.'

Mabel shrugged again. 'Things,' she said. 'Things I want to do.'

'Why?' asked Wonder.

'To be free,' said Mabel.

Wonder looked into the eyes of her new friend. 'I will help you,' she said.

7 Hollowbeak's warning

Wonder and Hollowbeak sat together on the emerald lawn at the perimeter of Direleafe Hall.

Though it was late, the stars and moon were bright and the dewdrops clinging to the blades of grass were like trembling fireflies. Above their heads, night birds circled. But Hollowbeak stayed with Wonder. *Why did you choose to be punished?* he asked. *Why are you helping her?*

'Because Mabel is my *friend,*' Wonder

replied. 'I want to be with her.'

She won't appreciate it. No matter what you do, no matter how you try to prove it to her, she will leave you. Everyone leaves you. I look after you, Wonder. I protect you. I am the only one who stays.

'Maybe I don't want you to stay,' Wonder said, quietly, 'if you are always so gloomy.'

Wonder stood. She picked up her long skirt and began the climb up the hill, back to Direleafe Hall. She held a haphazard bunch of wildflowers. She had been out all night, picking them for Mabel.

After the punishment, she hadn't felt like going back to the archives. She hadn't felt like lying down, in the nook beside that old, rusted cabinet, beneath that blanket – no matter how *fancy* it had seemed when Mabel was there.

She hadn't felt like sleeping. She worried that she would dream about something that wasn't Mabel, and that felt like a waste.

Hollowbeak stayed with her all night and she was glad of his company. But now, in the dawning light, as tiredness began to rake its bony fingers through her mind, she was growing weary of him. He only wanted to tell her, over and over, how terrible Mabel was. But Wonder knew it wasn't true.

The sun rose over Direleafe Hall, turning it from charcoal to copper and gold. From a gothic castle to a storybook palace.

Wonder sucked in a breath. She loved this moment – the moment when night finally surrendered to glorious day.

Night had its own beauty. Night had

the diamond stars and the perfect velvet blackness. But day ... day was life. Day was hope. And in the dawning hours, hope overcame darkness.

Wonder had always believed in hope. And what had it given her?

Mabel.

I am not always gloomy, said Hollowbeak, flying to land on her shoulder.

'You sound gloomy,' said Wonder, 'when you say that.'

Hollowbeak sighed. Through a tightly clamped beak, he mumbled an apology. Of sorts.

'What was that?' Wonder prompted.

Hollowbeak couldn't bring himself to say it again. So, instead, he changed the subject. *Sometimes, at night, you call for your mother.*

‘I miss her,’ Wonder said, simply, after a pause.

I am here now, Hollowbeak said. *I have always been here. I take care of you.*

‘Sometimes,’ Wonder said, ‘I don’t want you to. Sometimes, I know my own mind.’

You can control your mind, Hollowbeak snapped, *but you cannot control your heart, and therein lies the danger. Hearts can break, easy as the snapping of twigs.*

Wonder looked up at the trees. At the branches. She wondered, if she leaped onto one of those branches, if it would break. She wondered what it would feel like to make that happen – to *affect* the world around her and make a thing that was whole into something that was in pieces.

You’re thinking about things I don’t

mean you to think of, said Hollowbeak, grumpily. *I tell you these things because I love you. I don't want you to get hurt. You're not taking this seriously. This is your* life, *Wonder.*

'Yes,' said Wonder, defiantly, as she marched into the darkness of Direleafe Hall. 'Yes, Hollowbeak, it *is.*'

8

A surprise from the sky

Wonder and Mabel sat on the stone front steps of Direleafe Hall.

A chill wind blew across the grounds, towards them. The silver birches swayed like ghostly maidens. Hollowbeak's favourite creaked and moaned and danced only under duress, in a bent and fitful sort of way.

The sky was white in places and, in others, black and glowering. The clouds seemed heavy with the weight of all that was sorrowful in the world.

In opened windows, in Direleafe Hall, net curtains fluttered, like cobwebs full of moths. Even the bright green grass was moving, moving, moving to the whispered song on the wind.

Mabel drew her cardigan tight, so tight that Wonder could see her ribs. For some reason, this made Wonder's belly twist.

Mabel was so *human*. Beneath her skin there was a heart beating, and blood, and lungs expanding and contracting – all of it like a clockwork and with its own kind of rhythmic dance that seemed, at that moment, so tenuous.

As if the wind might suddenly drop.

And then the dance would stop.

When Mabel breathed out, it was silver smoke, and her nose was red with the cold, like a berry-lipped elf had kissed her there.

And Wonder wished she had a handkerchief to give; was, in fact, searching her pockets for one ... when the paint can fell from the sky.

The paint was black as tar, blacker than the blackest parts of the sky. It was sticky, too, and it coated Mabel like a robber's cloak. 'Oh, dillweed!' Mabel cried.

She was wet with it. Wet and shaking and shivering as the paint can fell to the ground like a slap and both girls jumped and screamed, until Mabel looked up.

And so did Wonder.

Together the friends looked at the sky, from where the paint can had fallen, and, behind a cobweb curtain, inside an open window, there floated the snickering grin of Georgiana Kinch.

Wonder growled, ‘I’ll break her bones,’ and she would have, but Mabel shook her head.

‘No,’ she said, simply. ‘That’s not on my list.’

'What can we do, then?' asked Wonder.

Mabel wiped away some of the black paint, revealing the pale skin below, and she smiled. 'I think I will wash,' she said, simply. 'And then, I believe, I shall need a hairpin. For today, I might be a thief.'

'You have a thief's cloak,' said Wonder, chancing a joke.

And, to her relief, Mabel threw back her head and laughed a laugh made of silver smoke and wonderful wickedness.

'I do,' she said. 'It's perfect. And I'm glad that this has happened.'

'Why?' asked Wonder, bemused.

'I needed an excuse,' said Mabel, 'an excuse to be bad.'

9

Thieves

Wonder and Mabel stood in the cloakroom. It was a damp and dreary space – the ceiling was thick with mould and the floor was a mess of puddles, even when it wasn't raining. The morning dew must creep in there, Wonder always thought, when it was too cold to stay outside.

The middle of the room was taken up by wooden racks for coats, and the walls were lined with tall metal lockers. Not all of the girls had a locker – most kept their books in their rooms and lugged them down the many stairs before classes, and then up again afterwards. But some girls had parents with money, and these girls kept their things locked away in this room, downstairs, and never had to lug at all.

'Do you know which one is hers?' asked Mabel.

Wonder nodded. She knew every inch of Direleafe Hall. 'That one,' she said, pointing.

Mabel rolled her eyes. She gave a little cough that became a laugh. 'I should have known.'

Georgiana's locker was the only one with little red hearts all over it. And in the centre of the metal door was a picture of Georgiana and all her friends.

Wonder used to look at the picture

with envy. Now, she saw it through Mabel's eyes. 'It is a little bit silly, isn't it?' Wonder said, laughing.

Mabel nodded. And then she skipped across to the locker and traced the edges of the picture with her fingers.

'You're going to steal that?' Wonder gasped.

Mabel shook her head. She pointed at the hairpin in Wonder's hand. 'Do you know how to use it?'

A grin spread slowly over Wonder's face. She nodded. 'I do.'

Her smile drooped a little bit as she remembered when she had learned the skill, helped by Hollowbeak, who seemed to possess knowledge of a disturbing number of criminal talents.

Just a little bit that way, he'd told her, as she'd wiggled the pin in the rusty lock of the archives room's ancient cabinet. *Listen for the click.*

It hadn't taken very long for the click to sound. It hadn't taken very long, either, to find the mildewed folder inside.

And it hadn't taken very long to read it.

There wasn't much of a story. There hadn't been enough time, she supposed, to make a longer one.

She shook her head, shook the memory out of her. It floated away like a dandelion head.

'I'll teach you,' she said to Mabel. 'You just listen for the click ...'

Mabel was a very fast learner. In a matter of minutes, Georgiana's locker popped open, breathing out vanilla perfume.

'What will you take?' asked Wonder.

Mabel smiled and reached inside the shadowy depths. She retrieved a small pink envelope. She opened it and, while Wonder watched, she read the contents.

Mabel looked up at Wonder with sparkling eyes. 'It's a love note,' she said.

'Who is it for?' asked Wonder, eagerly.

Mabel shook her head.

Wonder deflated. 'What are you going to do with it?' she asked, in a small voice.

'Just ... take it,' Mabel said.

'Not ... tell everyone?' Wonder asked.

Mabel met her eyes. 'No,' she said. 'I only wanted to steal. If I told everyone ... that would be a different thing. That would be nasty. I am not nasty. All of this was a little bit *bad*, it's true, but it wasn't ever nasty.'

She slid the letter into the pocket of her cardigan. And then she closed the locker door.

'Won't you tell me who it was for?' Wonder asked, as they walked away.

Mabel looked through the window, out into the grounds and to the tree where Hollowbeak sat. 'I can trust you?' she said. 'You won't tell anyone?'

Wonder followed Mabel's gaze over to Hollowbeak. She turned away, blocking him out so she could see only her friend. 'You can trust me.'

Mabel leaned close and whispered a name.

Wonder's eyes widened. 'I promise I won't tell a soul,' she whispered. 'You can trust me completely.'

Mabel nodded. She pulled a piece of paper from her cardigan pocket.

Not Georgiana's letter – that was safely folded away. This was the paper with the list. She smoothed it flat. Then she crossed out the first line.

~~Steal something~~

10
Dreaming

That night, Wonder lay in her attic bed. And she dreamed. And it was glorious.

She dreamed that she and Mabel stood in front of the class, dressed in top hats and tails, dancing and singing to the delight of everyone.

Ms Gallow smiled.

Hollowbeak – who sat at the window – bobbed along to the jolly song they sang.

Even Georgiana Kinch's face, when

it was not tarnished by meanness, was curiously lovely.

Wonder's mother was there, as she always was in Wonder's dreams, right in the middle of everything. Happy. Radiant. Full of life and love and *everything.*

And she looked like Wonder – that dark hair and those dark eyes and that smile that made dents in her cheeks – but she *glowed.* She glowed more than Wonder ever had. She was lit from within. She was the most beautiful person Wonder had ever seen.

Then.

Now.

She smiled at Wonder and she beckoned, and Wonder wanted more than anything to run into her arms.

But she knew she couldn't. It wasn't

time. There was something she had to *do* first. But what was it?

Usually, Wonder woke from these dreams, upset and shivering. Because she could not run into her mother's arms. Because her mother did not exist. Because her mother *did* exist, somewhere ...

Somewhere far away.

But Wonder could not go to her.

She was trapped, here, so heavy and stuck, and she did not know how to be light. She did not know how to be free.

Hollowbeak would hop onto her knee and lean his downy head on her chest and stroke her gently with his wing until her breathing calmed. They would sit that way until things were ...

Not good, but better, at least.

This time, in this dream, Wonder did

not feel sad or worried. She knew she was doing exactly what she was meant to be doing.

Dancing with Mabel.

It wasn't enough to make her light. It wasn't enough to make her free. But it was something.

Wonder, in the dream, was something.

Wonder Quinn was always a background kind of girl, even before. But it never used to matter. She'd always had her mother and her mother was Wonder's best friend. Her mother was everything.

Maybe the other girls saw that, before. They saw there was no space for them. And that was true.

Wonder's mother sang to her and they danced and they laughed, up in their attic quarters. They danced so hard the floorboards creaked and the golden motes rose up to dance with them, and Wonder had all she needed, then.

But since her mother left ...

There had been a hole. Or maybe there was always a hole, but her mother had obscured it.

Wonder had not danced, since her mother left her. There was nobody to dance with.

Until Mabel.

And now she danced with Mabel, and Mabel filled the hole, and everything seemed to be more *right* than it had been for a long time, or maybe than it had ever been.

It was almost completely right.

It was almost completely perfect.

Almost.

11
Telling truths

At lunchtime, Wonder Quinn and Mabel Clattersham sat on the roof of Direleafe Hall.

On the emerald grass below, girls sat in circles gossiping, or played with jumping ropes and balls. Wonder and Mabel paid them no attention. They were thinking of bigger things.

From his perch on the silver birch tree, Hollowbeak watched the both of them. His eyes were narrowed and his wings crossed in front of him like folded arms. The girls paid him no mind, either. They were in a bubble, only big enough for two.

'You know you'll get in trouble if Ms Gallow sees you up here,' Wonder warned Mabel, though her heart wasn't in it, really. The last thing she wanted was for Mabel to leave, and she was secretly glad when Mabel only shrugged.

'I don't mind. What about you? Do you ever get in trouble?' asked Mabel.

'They don't notice me,' Wonder said, quietly, picking her fingernail.

'I don't know how that could be possible,' said Mabel. 'You caught my eye the moment I walked into the classroom. I knew I had to sit next to you and be your friend. You seemed like you were infinite. You're extraordinary, Wonder Quinn.'

Wonder, in that moment, felt exactly that. 'Thank you,' she whispered.

'Why do you think they don't notice you?' Mabel tugged at the corner of a shingle that was lifting. She prised off a chunk that was shaped like a heart and gave it to Wonder.

Wonder thought it was the most beautiful thing she had ever seen – much more beautiful than Georgiana's gaudy love-hearts. She put it in her pocket, with the blunt pencil. They were her treasures.

'They don't notice me because they don't know how to,' said Wonder. 'Because I have no parents and no home. They don't want to admit I'm real because that means that horrible things happen to real people in the real world, and horrible things might happen to them. They don't want to admit that heartbreak is a fact.'

'Are you heartbroken, then?' asked Mabel.

Wonder shook her head. 'It's not broken,' she said. 'But it should be. It should be in a thousand pieces or more. I should have drowned the world with my tears, but they are all still inside me. I don't know how to cry them.'

There was a broken beat and both girls looked away, one down and one up, and both at nothing, really.

'Your mother is dead?' said Mabel, at last.

Wonder nodded. 'She died in a fire,' she said. 'She was a teacher here, at Direleafe Hall. We had our own room. The fire ate everything.'

'She died but you survived,' said Mabel.

Wonder looked away again.

'You're like me,' Mabel said, after it was clear Wonder would not speak. 'I don't cry, ever. My mother says my nerves are all on the outside of my skin. She says I feel too much – too deeply. But she's wrong. I feel all sorts of things. But not sorrow. My mother banned sorrow when I was small and now, I don't know how to feel it. She does, though. My mother is all sorrow. Not in front of me, of course, but when her bedroom door is locked, when she thinks I can't hear.'

'One day, I will cry,' whispered Wonder. 'And on that day, I will break apart and float off to the stars. I am too heavy, now, to float.'

'You speak like a poem,' said Mabel. 'You speak in riddles. You are a riddle,

Wonder Quinn. A beautiful, golden riddle. I wonder, sometimes, if there isn't a dragon guarding you – if you aren't, in truth, a treasure.' Mabel looked away, into the clouds. '*That* one looks like a dragon,' she said, pointing.

'That one looks like a walrus,' said Wonder, giggling.

'Do you think I could jump from here to the branch?' Mabel looked at the silver birch tree and then back at Wonder. 'I'd like to do that, I think. Like Tarzan. A *wild thing.* Could I make it, do you think?'

'Yes,' Wonder said, firmly. 'I've done it a thousand times. It's only a small distance. Look. There's Hollowbeak. See how close he is? You could almost touch him, if you reached out far enough. But if you jump, for a moment – a tiny moment between the roof and the tree – it is as if you're just ...'

'In the sky?'

'In the sky,' Wonder said, nodding.

'I just have to leap.'

'You just have to leap. And believe.'

Mabel pushed herself into a crouch. 'Well, then,' she said. 'Wish me luck.'

12

After Mabel leaped

They sat by the base of the tree, nestled in the soft, soft grass like two flowers, blooming.

Mabel crossed another line from her list. The line was a little bit shaky.

~~Leap into the sky.~~

Wonder wanted to hold her hand to steady the pencil.

Wonder wanted to hold her hand.

'I'm breathing so quickly,' said Mabel.

'Because you are frightened?'

'Because I have too much breath for my body. I have too much *everything* for my body. I am too much. That was too much.'

'It was bad?'

Mabel shook her head. She leaned back against the branch of the tree.

'You flew,' said Wonder, and both girls closed their eyes. Wonder remembered Mabel soaring through the air.

It had been safe. Wonder had known it would be safe. She never would have chanced Mabel's life. She never would have let her fly if she'd imagined she might fall.

But it still felt dangerous, what Mabel did, in the way that all beautiful things are dangerous.

Wonder opened her eyes and looked

at Mabel. Her friend's eyes were pressed shut, still, and Wonder found she could not imagine what Mabel was thinking. It made her arms prickle. Within her, a rubber band pulled tight. To snap it, she said, 'You're a marvel, Mabel.'

'Am I?' Mabel replied. But she didn't open her eyes as she spoke again. 'Tell me about you, Wonder. While I find my breath and my strength. Tell me five things that make you *Wonder Quinn*.'

Wonder thought for a very long time. She had to remember *hard.* And then, finally, as Mabel stayed so silent and still as if she were a statue, she said, 'I am Wonder. I love to dance and to laugh, but I hadn't done much of either for a very long time, before I met you.'

'That's about *me*,' Mabel interrupted. 'Tell me about *you*.'

'All right,' said Wonder. She lifted her eyes heavenward. 'I like to dance – I told you that. And I like the colour blue. The kind where it's blue like blueberries. The kind where it's trying to be purple, but just not quite getting there. I like the sound of piano being played in another room, like it's a memory of song, echoing through the years. I like dandelions that push through the dirt a week before it's springtime. And I ...'

She scrunched her eyes closed. That was only four and Mabel had said *five.* But Wonder couldn't think of another, all on her own, so she borrowed one of Mabel's.

'*I am infinite,*' she whispered.

Mabel smiled. Without opening her eyes, she nodded. 'All of us are,' she said. 'But only some of us know it. Thank you for telling me your things, Wonder Quinn. I like you even more now.'

Above the two girls, Hollowbeak snorted. Wonder ignored him.

'Can I hold your hand?' asked Mabel.

Wonder felt as if she was full of beetles. She knew she should say no. But she said *yes*.

Mabel reached out. Her fingers on Wonder's skin were like tears of laughter.

'I feel like I'm touching a star,' said Mabel.

'I am so happy,' said Wonder. And the truth of those words was as solid as the earth beneath her.

Mabel took out her pencil and crossed two items off her list.

~~Touch a star.~~

~~Make someone feel pure happiness.~~

Her crossings were even shakier this time.

'I'm getting through it too quickly,' she whispered. 'Much too quickly.'

13
Confrontation

Mabel and Wonder sat again in the library, in the soft, quiet time at the end of the day. Wonder was showing Mabel all her favourite books.

The Silver-eyed Girl

The Winged Heart

Ink and Bones

The Tale of Boundless Joy

'How have you read so many books?' asked Mabel.

'I've had a lot of time,' answered Wonder.

'Do you take them upstairs to your little room?' asked Mabel.

Wonder nodded. 'I read there by candlelight. I like the way the candlelight looks on the pages. It makes it seem as if the book is alive. The words dance up into the air and into my soul.'

'I want to read every book in the world,' said Mabel. 'I want to know everything everyone has ever said.'

'You could,' said Wonder, grinning.

'Will you do it for me?' said Mabel.

She looked at the library clock. 'Oh, dillweed. I have to go. My parents will be waiting. I hate the end of these days.'

'So do I,' said Wonder.

As they walked together out of the library, a tall, thin girl with snow-pale hair – who was not like a snake but a kitten, pretending – stepped into Mabel's path. 'You took my letter,' she spat.

'I don't know what you mean,' said Mabel.

If Wonder hadn't known the truth, she would have believed Mabel. Mabel knew how to lie. She was good at it and this made Wonder feel a bit sad.

'I know it was you. My friend Alice saw you go into the cloakroom.' Georgiana gave Mabel a push in the chest. It was only a small push, but a moment later, Mabel was on the floor.

Georgiana ran away.

Wonder held Mabel's hand again, as she breathed in and out, in and out, more and more quickly.

'Not enough air,' gasped Mabel.

14

Mabel was not there

Wonder sat with Hollowbeak on the wall by the school gate.

All the other girls had filed into the hall already.

Mabel was not there.

Mabel was late.

Mabel was not coming.

The afternoon before, when Georgiana pushed her, when she fell, when she couldn't get air, Ms Gallow had come running. She had pulled Mabel away from Wonder without a word and carried her off down the hallway.

Wonder had watched as Mabel's parents ran in through the gate.

Mabel's father had cradled her in his arms, like she was a baby, and Wonder realised, for the first time since that first day, how small Mabel really was. She seemed so big when she was awake, when she was talking and laughing and making jokes.

An ambulance had arrived moments later, and Mabel and her dad had disappeared inside.

I told you she would leave, Hollowbeak said to Wonder.

Wonder did not reply.

She knew the truth. She felt it. Mabel was gone but Mabel would come back. She knew and felt it, deep in her bones. Mabel was still there, still tethered to her – her heart tied to Wonder's with an iron chain.

Hollowbeak stroked her cheek with his feathers. It felt nice. But not as nice as when Mabel held her hand.

15
Remembering

Wonder sat in her room.

The candle was burning down, down, and the shadows made pictures on the wall that looked like hand puppets acting out memories.

Of Wonder. Of her mother. Of both of them, here, in this room, in this very spot, watching shadows on the wall by candlelight.

Holding hands.

Wonder could still remember the last time they did that. It was always the time she felt the safest – when her mother was holding her hand. As if all was right with the world. As if no bad things could ever happen.

As if nobody could ever die ...

Wonder didn't see her mother die.

It was too bright in the room. It blinded her. And then it was too dark, from all the smoke.

It was loud, too, but she heard her mother over the noise. She didn't scream and she didn't cry.

She sang.

'My small, precious hatchling,
In your nest, tucked in tight,
Flutter down your eyelids
And bid the stars goodnight ...'

And she sang it again and again and again, until she ...

Stopped.

Wonder didn't see her mother die. She only heard it when she *stopped*.

She didn't scream and she didn't cry.

She felt heavy. The ceiling fell down around her and she was so heavy she couldn't move.

She was heavy, still, after all this time.

And she thought, at the time, *If only I could cry. My tears would put out this fire and we would all be saved.*

But she could not cry and she could not put out the fire.

She couldn't save anyone.

16
A whole week

Wonder walked the corridors of Direleafe Hall. She sat on its rooftop and on its emerald grass. She sat in her chair in Ms Gallow's classroom and she lay in her attic bed, and hours passed and then days and none of it felt real.

Mabel was gone. Mabel was *gone.*

Wonder did not sleep.

Wonder did not smile.

Wonder barely listened when Hollowbeak spoke to her.

She lost herself in books, in the back of

the library. They were her only comfort.

The Silver-eyed Girl

The Winged Heart

And she found a new one, about a girl who was a warrior, who saved the entire world. Wonder tried to imagine what that would be like. To be able to *change* things like that. To be brave like that. She tried to imagine herself dressed in armour – roaring, *fighting*.

When she was with Mabel, it felt possible. *She* felt possible.

Her mother had always told her that she should find her own power within herself, that she should love herself first, and that no other human should make her feel lesser or more.

But Wonder imagined herself as a sputtering candle – years and dust and greyness had nearly put her out. Her power and love for herself had dimmed.

But then a girl with sparks in her eyes had come and she had touched her, and Wonder had felt it – for the first time in many years – the possibility of light.

When Mabel was with her, she did feel infinite. She felt like she could roar.

But Mabel was not here, now.

Could Wonder still roar, without her?

Maybe.

Maybe she would try, soon.

But in the meantime, she read about girls who could, and about all manner of other things: dragons and monsters and demons and angels and all of the world.

She read for Mabel, who wanted to read everything. She read in the archives room, while her candle flickered. She even read in her lessons.

She only stopped, sometimes, to

watch Ms Gallow's writing waft across the blackboard like smoke. She copied some of the quotes into her workbook, with Mabel's blunt pencil.

Let my heart be still a moment and
this mystery explore;—
'Tis the wind and nothing more!

That's from Poe's 'The Raven', Hollowbeak whispered. He was hiding below Wonder's desk.

'I know,' said Wonder, and she thought of Mabel and her riddle about the writing desk.

Stop thinking about her, said Hollowbeak. *She isn't coming back.*

But Hollowbeak was wrong and Wonder was right, because Mabel did come back.

She came back after an entire week.

And she brought with her a large mince pie.

17
The pie

Georgiana Kinch sat with Alice and Jemima and Amelia and Eloise in the most coveted spot in the schoolyard.

The steps that led to the main entrance were out of bounds to all but Georgiana's group before school, at morning break and at lunchtime.

Everyone knew that.

Even though Mabel was new, she knew that.

That's why, on the morning she arrived back at Direleafe Hall, she went straight there.

Her parents waved her goodbye from the school gates. They watched as she marched into the schoolyard and made sure she was safe. They called out to her, 'We love you.'

Mabel waved at them and called back, 'Go now. I mean it. I'm fine.'

As they walked back to their car, Wonder saw they never took their eyes off Mabel. Wonder didn't, either. She stared, unblinking, down at her friend, and her smile was as big as the sky.

Mabel's shoulders were back. Her chin was high. She looked straight ahead. Straight at the steps to Direleafe Hall.

'You were wrong,' Wonder told Hollowbeak.

I wasn't wrong, he replied. *It's only that I wasn't right,* yet.

As Hollowbeak huffed and flounced away, Wonder watched as Mabel walked up to Georgiana. She watched as Mabel reached into her leather knapsack. She watched as Mabel extracted the pie.

Wonder's heart stopped as she remembered the line that Mabel had written:

Throw a pie.

She watched as the smirk on Georgiana's face slowly melted away.

And she remembered how Mabel had picked the lock and taken the letter, and Wonder knew that Mabel could be bad, that Mabel *could* throw a pie in a mean girl's face, and that maybe Georgiana deserved it, but ...

She found that she didn't want Mabel to do it. Because Mabel wasn't nasty and throwing a pie *was*.

And Mabel held the pie high.

And Georgiana flinched.

And Mabel drew her arm back ...

And Wonder could not breathe.

And then ...

Then, Mabel looked up at Wonder and Wonder shook her head. *No!*

And Mabel ... stopped.

She stopped and said something to Georgiana that Wonder could not hear, then she threw the pie down so it smashed on the grey cobblestones.

And then she walked away towards Direleafe Hall, towards Wonder.

Wonder skittered down the shingles. She leaped through the sky – so wide and vast and intensely, stubbornly grey – into the tree that Hollowbeak loved. She skipped through the branches onto the soft, dewy grass, and she ran, faster than she ever had before, all the way over to her friend. She wrapped her arms around her and she whispered in her ear, 'I missed you, I missed you, I missed you.'

'I did the pie,' said Mabel. 'I threw the pie.'

'But not at Georgiana,' Wonder pointed out.

'No,' said Mabel. 'But I could have. And she knew it. And she fears me now.'

'What did you tell her?' Wonder asked Mabel. 'What did you say?'

Mabel lifted a shoulder. 'I said I didn't care. I didn't care what Georgiana thought because I am infinite and she is small. And she will always be small, but very soon I will have the whole universe.'

'What does that mean?' asked Wonder, but Mabel didn't reply.

Instead, Mabel took Wonder's hand and they walked together into Direleafe Hall. They walked together into Ms Gallow's classroom and they sat together, side by side, holding hands, waiting for their punishment.

Because Mabel had not thrown the pie at Georgiana, but she knew she would be punished, still, and that was almost the point.

And they were both perfectly happy.

18

More punishment

Ms Gallow sat behind her desk, like a magistrate, presiding. She shook her head at Mabel. 'What were you thinking?' she asked.

Mabel stared back, smiling, calm. 'I was thinking,' she said, 'that Georgiana Kinch deserved a pie in her face.'

'For what crime?' asked Ms Gallow. 'I know she pushed you ... but she didn't *know*, Mabel.'

'I know that. And I probably deserved the push. But I wanted ... I just *so* wanted to do the pie. I tried to think, while I was lying in my bed, bored out of my mind, what person here would recover best from a pie in her face. And Georgiana Kinch ... she has so many friends. I knew her friends would wipe her clean.

'I knew that she would probably cry and they would probably hold her and brush away her tears and tell her how *very sorry* they were that this had happened, and they would, perhaps, maybe, even buy her chocolates. They would do all they could to make me a villain and Georgiana a hero and, so, it would turn out so much better for Georgiana, in the end.'

'But you did not throw the pie at Georgiana, in the end.'

'She didn't deserve to be a hero,' said Mabel, simply.

She took a breath, finally, and it was a jagged, wavering thing, but somehow brave.

Wonder brushed her hand down her friend's arm. Mabel, she thought, *was* a superhero. An avenger. A brave, brilliant creature who could throw pies at girls like Georgiana Kinch but didn't.

Mabel lifted her chin. She looked right in Ms Gallow's eyes and said, 'I'm sorry about the pie mess on the cobblestones, though. Sorrier, perhaps, than I would have been about Georgiana's face. I'll clean them. But there should be more. More punishment. What is my punishment, Ms Gallow?'

Ms Gallow stared at Mabel for the longest time, for a stretched-elastic moment.

Wonder did not breathe.

Then, Ms Gallow sighed. And she said, 'I used to go to this school, did you know? I was so afraid when I was here, all the time. Especially of girls like Georgiana Kinch.'

She lifted one corner of her mouth. 'There was one girl, in particular. Her name was Abigail. I would have liked to put a pie in her face. I think I would have chosen a blueberry one. And maybe I wouldn't have been as good as you. Maybe I would have *done* it.'

She shook her head, smiling, as if imagining her old foe, face stained with indigo juice and anger. And then she gave a little snort that sounded not unlike Hollowbeak.

She wiped at the corner of one of her eyes with her index finger and then tapped on the board with her chalk. 'Right,' she said. 'Punishment.' She shook her head. 'Life is too short for punishment, isn't it?' She smiled at Mabel, and Wonder knew that *she* knew about Mabel's list. 'But you like writing, don't you?'

Mabel nodded. 'Amongst other things.'

'Write me something, then,' said Ms

Gallow. 'Just a few lines. About whatever you like.'

'Do I have to show it to you?' asked Mabel.

Ms Gallow seemed to consider it. Finally, she shook her head. 'No. You don't have to show me.'

Wonder turned to Mabel when Ms Gallow had turned to her reading. 'Will you show me?' she asked.

Mabel nodded. 'I will show you.'

Wonder felt as if Mabel had agreed to show her soul.

'Should I write something, too?' she asked Mabel.

'I would love that,' said Mabel.

19
Mabel's poem

This is what Mabel wrote:

Life is too tiny
For lines,
For boxes,
For smallness ...
Life is too enormous
For small people like me
To make even a tiny mark on it.
But a bird, flying through the clouds,
Makes no mark on the earth and yet,
Is happy,

Is free,
And it looks, when you see it next to a star,
The very same size.
I am a bird.
I am happy now.
I am free.

20
Wonder's poem

This is what Wonder wrote:

I have a friend.
She came from the stars.
She is bigger than the universe.
But she wants to sit beside me
Even though I am grey.
She likes me
Even though I am not one tiny bit
As bright as she is.
She is my friend
And it is the very best thing.

21 Candlelight shadows

Wonder sat beneath her blanket in the archives room. Her candle was still alight, but she had put her book down on the dusty floor beside her perhaps an hour before.

She watched as the candlelight made shadows, again, in the labyrinth of cracks in the ceiling above her. They looked like people, navigating the maze. As she let her eyes lose focus, she imagined they were people she knew.

There was Ms Gallow, tall and bony,

her nose like a raven's beak.

Georgiana was there, as well, her face stormy, her eyes lightning bolts.

There were other girls, too, from this year and the ones before. Some she had liked. Some she had wished were her friends.

There was Genevieve, who had hair she wore in braids all the way down to her waist, who sounded like Snow White when she sang, who only ever ate marmalade sandwiches for lunch.

There was Evangeline, whose father was a vicar, who could recite whole pages from the Bible, who drew naughty pictures in the back cover of her workbook.

Then, last year, there was Lily, who looked like a Christmas angel, who sang to herself, who always stuck her tongue out when she used scissors, who liked to read in the library, too.

Sometimes, Wonder sat beside her and they read together, but Lily never looked at her or said a single word.

All of them were wished-for friends, but they weren't real ones. Not like Mabel.

Wonder saw her now, a candlelight shadow wandering into the maze. She was slower than the others, and smaller. She didn't run. Sometimes, she had to stop for a rest.

But that was all right, because Wonder was in the maze with her, walking by her side. The bigger shadows that looked scary never came near the two friends because Wonder protected Mabel from all the darkness.

In the middle of the labyrinth, Wonder saw a woman. She was small and still, watching her. On the woman's shoulder there sat a crow.

Wonder closed her eyes. When she opened them again, the shadow-people were gone.

She let her eyes rest on the locked filing cabinet in the corner of the archives.

A dagger scraped across her chest as she remembered that file and the tiny story contained within it. The one that ended so suddenly, without so much as a line or two to make an epilogue.

With a shiver, she used the palm of her hand to put out the candle. She didn't feel any burning.

As she closed her eyes again, she was sure she could hear a faint rustling in the ceiling above her. She imagined it was the shadow-people still searching for the centre of the maze.

22
Hollowbeak helps

Wonder and Mabel sat with Hollowbeak on the roof again. Wonder stared at Hollowbeak, intently, and Hollowbeak made a show of ignoring her.

Don't do that, said Hollowbeak, finally giving in. *I'm not helping.*

'Please, Hollowbeak?' Wonder asked.

The crow glowered at Mabel, and Mabel looked at Wonder with very wide eyes. 'What's he saying?' she asked.

'You see him, too?' Wonder asked, inclining her head to one side.

'Sometimes I wonder if he's even there at all. Nobody else can talk to birds.'

Not birds, Hollowbeak reminded her. *Bird. You can talk only to me.*

'We don't know that,' Wonder said. 'I've never tried talking to another bird. I could,' she said, bravely, 'if you're not nice to me.'

'I see him,' said Mabel. 'I see both of you, clear as day. What's he saying?'

Wonder looked at Hollowbeak, one eyebrow raised. A moment later, she looked at Mabel with a smile. 'He says he will help. He says he knows where to go.'

They followed Hollowbeak through one of the upper windows of Direleafe Hall.

'Inside?' asked Mabel.

Hollowbeak turned his head to give her a beady stare. *Inside*, he replied.

He hopped his way down the corridor. Students, on their way to class, passed the trio. They gave Mabel sideways, squinty looks. Everyone knew about the pie and everyone knew Ms Gallow had only given Mabel a few lines to write, instead of a proper punishment. They wondered why Mabel had thrown the pie at the ground, and not at Georgiana Kinch.

Everyone was now suspicious of Mabel Clattersham.

Mabel didn't seem to notice the stares, so intent she was on following Hollowbeak.

As they began climbing the spiral staircase, Wonder felt her belly twist. 'Hollowbeak,' she asked. 'Where are you taking us?'

The archives, he replied.

'My room?' Wonder asked, confused. 'There are no birds up there.'

There are, replied Hollowbeak. He did not say any more.

When they reached Wonder's room, Hollowbeak led them over to the corner. He pointed up with his beak, towards the rafters.

There, he said. *Can you see the nest of starlings?*

Wonder thought of the night before, when she had heard a faint rustling above her. She knew Hollowbeak was telling the truth.

'But how will we get up there?' she asked him.

It was Mabel who pointed at the locked filing cabinet. 'We could climb on that,' she said. Her eyes sparkled as she peered at Wonder. 'Maybe we should open it first, though. I know how to pick locks, now. We could open it and look inside.'

You could do that ... said Hollowbeak, casually.

Wonder began to back away. She shook her head. 'No!' she said to Hollowbeak. 'No. I won't do that. Not again. You tricked me, Hollowbeak.'

Hollowbeak said nothing. His stare had a smugness about it.

'You know I can't do that,' Wonder hissed. 'Not *ever* again. Why would you suggest it? You evil, evil bird.' She raised her voice. 'Get out!' she yelled. 'Get out of my room now, and never come back. I never want to see you again!'

Why are you so frightened? he asked. *Why are you so frightened of the truth?* Hollowbeak stared at her for a moment more. Then he lifted his onyx chin and flew away out the window.

'It's all right,' said Mabel, flying to Wonder's side. 'It's all right. I'm sorry. I'm sorry, Wonder.'

And she held Wonder in her arms.

She *held Wonder*.

23 Wonder's secret

The girls remained enfolded together, standing in Wonder's room that, for a moment, felt much bigger than it truly was.

Wonder wished to never let go, and she mightn't, if Mabel hadn't gently moved away. 'It's all right,' said Mabel, taking a step back. 'I don't need to hold the bird. It's a silly thing. The whole ...' She coughed and placed a hand against her chest. 'The whole list is a silly thing,' she finished weakly.

Mabel wobbled a little bit. Wonder reached out to catch her, but she wasn't quick enough. Mabel fell to the floor.

'Oh, dillweed!' Wonder gasped. 'What's wrong?'

Mabel curled into a little ball of bones and softness. She tucked her knobbly knees to her chest and gave a quiet moan. 'I'm sorry, Wonder. I made you upset. I made you lose your friend.'

'That's all right,' Wonder said, stroking her friend's hair. 'I have you now.'

Mabel shook her head. There were tears on her cheeks. 'I'm not going to be here for long, Wonder.'

Wonder didn't want to believe it, but in her heart of hearts she knew it was true. Maybe she had always known. Just like she knew why she could talk to Hollowbeak, and why Mabel believed she could.

Her mother had told her, once, about what crows really are. And what they mean. And why only some people can see them.

Hollowbeak was right. Mabel was going to leave her.

'That's what the list is about, isn't it?' she asked, softly. 'You're sick. You want to do those things because you might have to leave.'

'They're the only things I really want to do,' Mabel whispered. 'The only things I planned to do, before I came here. That and make a friend. I did that already.' She smiled up at Wonder. 'I think I can sit now,' she said.

Wonder nodded. Mabel pushed herself up.

'The bird thing is ... fine, though.' She patted Wonder's arm. 'It was the least important thing. If you can't go near the cabinet ... for whatever reason.'

'It has my secret in it,' Wonder said, looking at her friend with prickling eyes. 'I read it, once and I ... I hate even thinking about it. If I don't think about it, it might not be true. It might not be real.' She shook her head. 'It's a silly thing. I know I won't see it again if I go near the cabinet but ... That's why I sleep up here. Just to make sure nobody else comes near it and nobody else knows. And it's ridiculous because nobody ever wants to come here. They never want to see the cabinet because it's only full of ancient stories and nobody seems to want those any more.'

'It's all right. Really,' said Mabel.

She didn't ask Wonder's secret.

Wonder hoped maybe it was because

she was her friend. And friends don't ask. Friends wait for you to tell.

But Wonder thought maybe that wasn't it at all. Maybe, in her heart of hearts, Mabel already knew.

And maybe that's what a friend was, actually.

Someone who already knows.

24
This moment, only

The two girls sat together, beneath the rough woollen blanket.

They knew it was time for lessons – the bell had already clanged. They knew that Ms Gallow would be cross. They knew there would probably be an actual punishment this time.

Ms Gallow did not abide students missing lessons.

Wonder and Mabel didn't care. About Ms Gallow. About lessons. About anything but *this.*

This moment. This moment, only.

They held, between them, inside their clasped-together hands, a baby bird.

It was the next thing on Mabel's list – her list of things she meant to do.

The baby bird was small and warm and so unimaginably fragile. It had a beak as yellow as dandelions and its feathers were black like Hollowbeak's, save for a fuzzy grey patch on its throat and on its tiny twig legs.

Its mother waited, anxiously, a foot away, pacing and cheeping soothingly to her baby.

It's all right, Hollowbeak assured her, for the twentieth time. *You can trust them.*

Wonder looked over at her friend with gratitude. After the way she'd spoken to him, she hadn't expected him to return, much less come back followed by the mother and the chick.

She should have known. Hollowbeak never left her. He was her constant. Her safety. He would be with her forever.

'Thank you,' Mabel whispered to the crow. 'Can you tell him?' she asked Wonder. 'Tell him, thank you?'

'He knows,' said Wonder. 'He understands.'

Mabel took out her piece of paper again. 'Will you cross out this line?' she asked Wonder. 'While I hold Pedro?'

'Who is Pedro?'

'The bird, silly,' said Mabel, laughing.

Wonder took Mabel's list. It was warm, from being in her pocket.

~~Steal something.~~
~~Leap into the sky.~~
~~Touch a star.~~
~~Make someone feel pure happiness.~~
~~Throw a pie.~~

And now ...

Wonder crossed out the second-last item:

~~Hold a baby bird.~~

'Only one more to go,' she said to her friend.

Break someone's heart.

Mabel nodded, blinking quickly. She looked down at the chick, stroked its soft head. It looked up at her, calmly. It knew she was good. 'It's so new,' she whispered. 'So perfectly new.'

Wonder reached over with a crooked finger and touched the small bird's chest. She could feel its heart, beating so quickly. *So few beats*, she thought. So few beats before the last one and they are going so quickly already.

'My mother and father want to take me away,' Mabel said, to Wonder. 'To a hospital. I don't want to go away. I want to keep coming to school. I want to stay with you a little while longer.'

Wonder nodded. 'I want that, too. But' – she gestured at the list – 'there's only one more thing. Does that mean ...'

Mabel grinned, her eyes shining. 'There is another thing, also,' she said. 'It isn't on the list.'

'Why?'

Mabel sighed. 'I didn't know ... I didn't know how far I'd get ... how I would ... *be*. I didn't know if I could. And I didn't want to fail.'

'What is it?'

Again, like she had with the name of Georgiana's sweetheart, Mabel leaned across to Wonder and whispered warm words in her ear.

'But you'd need to stay here at night-time,' Wonder said. 'Wouldn't your parents worry?'

'Don't you mind about them,' Mabel said. 'Will you do it with me?'

Wonder nodded. 'Anything,' she breathed. 'I'd do anything for you.'

Mabel smiled. 'I think I'd like to add to my poem now,' she said.

'Is it a poem about me?' Wonder asked, her eyes opening wide.

Mabel leaned her head to one side. 'Well,' she said, softly, 'I thought it was a poem about me, but perhaps it's about you, too. I started it when we were being punished, and then I wrote some more the next time we were being punished, but it never felt quite finished, and ... I like to finish things. Finishing things feels more urgent, now. More urgent by the day. Do you have paper?'

Wonder gave Mabel a piece of paper and Mabel gave Pedro to Wonder. And the mother bird – who was much braver than her size gave her cause at all to be – bobbed over to Wonder and cheeped, reproachfully.

Wonder was torn, for a moment. Should she give Pedro back to his mother, or was he happier here, in her hands?

In the end, Hollowbeak nudged her and said, *Go on. He's small. He needs his mother's love.*

Wonder felt a quick, sharp pain in her chest when he said that. But she passed Pedro back to his mother and his mother nudged him, protectively, with her beak, and they both seemed so happy that Wonder knew she had done the right thing. But she could still feel the shape of Pedro in her hands.

When Mabel finished writing, Wonder asked to read the poem, but Mabel shook her head.

'Not yet,' she said.

And then she said, 'But very soon, I think.'

25
Hollowbeak watched

Hollowbeak sat in the silver birch tree on a branch as slender as a bone.

As Hollowbeak watched, two girls ran through the darkness, shouting.

As Hollowbeak watched, the moonlight turned them both into stars.

As Hollowbeak watched, on their bare arms, tiny hairs stood on end. Even though one of them couldn't feel the cold. Even though one of them was no longer scared of anything.

Hollowbeak knew that Wonder was

frightened and wished he could swoop down and pluck out her fear as if it were a worm.

He loved Wonder and did not want her heart to break. Even though he had known, all along, that it would. Even though he knew he was right, he hadn't wanted to be.

And now, he knew there was nothing he could do.

The two girls wore only their short-sleeved nightdresses, so thin and flimsy that they might have been wearing nothing at all. When Hollowbeak had asked Wonder why Mabel wanted to do this – to run in the moonlight in only her nightclothes – Wonder had replied, 'Her mother and father never let her out at night. Her mother and father never let her run. She wants to be free.'

Hollowbeak felt a heavy stone inside his heart when Wonder said that. Because freedom is wonderful. Freedom is *life*, but it is also dangerous. It seemed, to Hollowbeak, that freedom – this time – was the thing that would break everything.

He wanted to forbid Wonder from doing this. He wanted to cage her, clip her wings, yell, *NO, Wonder!* and tell her of his fears ... But he knew, somehow, that doing that would mean losing her forever.

He knew that Wonder had to fly.

And perhaps ... perhaps this was the only way she could. Sometimes a twig has to break to force a bird to find their wings.

Hollowbeak sighed, then, the way he often did. He sighed for what he used to be. He sighed for what he could have been, if the fire hadn't eaten everything. What he and Wonder could have been. He used to shine so brightly, and now he was a strange, bent, twisted thing, but he loved her now as much as he always had.

Probably more.

As Hollowbeak watched, the two girls reached the limits of the grounds of Direleafe Hall.

He heard one of them – the one that wheezed and coughed and choked – cry out as best as her lungs could manage: 'I am free!'

And then, as Hollowbeak watched, she fell to the ground. To the soft, dewy, emerald grass.

And Hollowbeak heard Wonder howling.

And his heart did break, then. It broke for his darling girl.

26

Ms Gallow's discovery

In her tiny cottage behind Direleafe Hall, Ms Gallow heard Wonder howling, too.

It was the first time she'd ever heard her.

It would be the only time.

She dropped her knitting and put down her cup. She ran from her cottage, leaving the door wide open. She ran and ran and ran until she found the source of the sound.

There, she found a small, pale girl lying in the moonlight, shining like a star.

And her head, she noticed, was at a strange sort of angle. Almost as if it were being cradled in the arms of someone else.

But there was nobody there.

27
Wonder and Mabel

She breathed, for a little while. Small breaths – shallow and shuddering and so fragile, like the breaths of that baby bird.

And Wonder felt like the mother of the baby bird. So frightened and so protective and *so* full of love, and that was the thing, wasn't it? Love was so, so frightening. Because love was loss.

But she breathed, for a little while longer.

She breathed, while Ms Gallow

scooped her up and ran with her to Direleafe Hall.

She breathed, while the doctors came running, with their brown leather bags, stethoscopes flying behind them, reminding Wonder of the iron chain that still tethered her heart to Mabel's.

She breathed, while they set her down on the floor and pressed their mouths to hers and pushed on her small, bony chest and yelled words Wonder did not understand.

And Wonder wanted to tell them to stop because they would crack her bones, surely. They would crack her right open. And she knew that the clockwork inside Mabel Clattersham was broken, anyway, and the dance was ending.

She wished she could pick Mabel

up and dance with her until it ended, because Mabel would have liked that.

Mabel liked to dance.

But Wonder could only watch.

And she watched until Mabel did not breathe any more.

And it was only then that she left her, because she wasn't leaving at all.

Because Mabel had already gone.

28
Making marks

Wonder Quinn and Hollowbeak sat together on the roof of Direleafe Hall. Above them, the sky was stormy. The clouds seemed to contain an impossible ocean of unshed rain. It felt as if they might, at any moment, collapse under their own weight and fall down on the roof of Direleafe Hall and smash everything to pieces.

And this seemed entirely right. Entirely just.

It seemed, to Wonder, a marvel that

the whole world hadn't broken apart already.

Why were there still girls down there? Laughing, playing, running, *breathing*? Why was Georgiana Kinch down there, *existing*?

It wasn't right that the world continued when Mabel Clattersham did not.

Wonder reached into her pocket and pulled out a piece of paper. It wasn't the list – that did not matter any more. Perhaps it never had. It was not Georgiana's love letter.

It was another piece of paper, filled to the edges with small, elegant letters, made by Mabel Clattersham's small, pale hand.

It was Mabel's poem.

She had finished it.

Life is too tiny
For lines,
For boxes,
For smallness ...
Life is too enormous
For small people like me
To make even a tiny mark on it.
But a bird, flying through the clouds,
Makes no mark on the earth and yet,
Is happy,
Is free,
And it looks, when you see it next to a star,
The very same size.
I am like a bird.
I am happy now.
I am free.
And so is Wonder.
Wonder is more a bird than I will ever be.
Wonder deserves the whole universe.
I see her.

I love her.
Wonder deserves the sky.
She made a mark on me.
She gave me a full stop,
Perfectly round and whole.
I don't know if I made a mark on her.
I don't know if I gave her all she deserved.
But she gave me everything.
She gave me everything I needed.
She gave me my ending.
She is my Wonder.
The Wonder of my life.
And when she shines beside me,
I am infinite.
When we fly together, to the stars,
We are infinite.

'She did make a mark,' Wonder told Hollowbeak, as she folded the paper for the hundredth time and for the hundredth time slipped it back into her pocket. 'She made a mark like an earthquake makes a mark. Why could she not see that?'

Perhaps that is the beauty of humans, Hollowbeak said. *You make marks as big as earthquakes in the lives of those who love you, but you disappear without a trace. You were here and you were not here, all at once.*

'That's not beauty,' Wonder argued. 'That's tragedy.'

That's life, said Hollowbeak, simply. *All the beauty and all the tragedy ... so enormous when we're in it and when we're not ...*

'I still feel her,' Wonder whispered. 'I still feel her on my skin. So, you are wrong. We are enormous, always.'

29
After

Wonder Quinn sat in Ms Gallow's classroom. In front of her, the badger in the wood did not look quite so judgemental as it usually did. In fact, it looked quite sympathetic and sad. Wonder stroked its head. Funny old badger.

The lesson was about fairytales. She watched the chalk dance across the blackboard:

Back into the chamber turning, all my
soul within me burning,

Soon again I heard a tapping somewhat louder than before.

Her eyes left the board and wandered to the desk beside her.

And it was the absence of her that did it. The absence where once there had been so much. So much infinite *life.* And now there was nothing but air.

The absence of Mabel.

Now, that was a thing.

That was a thing so huge it felt like a universe, imploding.

It felt like Wonder's soul, imploding.

It felt like the last pieces of her heart, shattering.

After all this time.

Finally.

She breathed in.

She breathed out.

And then she left the classroom and walked up the stairs of Direleafe Hall.

She opened the door to the archives room and found her rough woollen blanket and the pile of books that sat beside it.

The Silver-eyed Girl

The Winged Heart

Ink and Bones

The Tale of Boundless Joy

And the one about the girl who was a warrior who roared, who saved the entire world.

She lit her candle and she read. She read and she read and, above her, though she did not glance up, in the middle of the shadow-maze, her mother waited with a crow on her shoulder.

And the candle flickered.

She let herself read all those beautiful

words and she was filled with all the miracles and all the sadness of the universe and tears spilled from her eyes.

And, after many hours and many tears, her eyelids fluttered and her book fell with a thud to the dusty floorboards, still dry, as if Wonder's tears had never fallen, as if Wonder had never been.

But she had.

She had been and she had lived, and she was golden and so light.

So beautifully light.

And she whispered to Hollowbeak and to the night, before she fell asleep: 'I am glad, in the end, that my heart broke, even though it was the worst thing in the world.'

And she dreamed of her mother, beckoning.

And she dreamed of Mabel, beckoning.

And she walked into their warm arms.

And that was a thing.

But the candle was still lit because she forgot to snuff it out, and it burned down and down and down. And then the very edge of one of the pages of the book that Wonder had dropped began to glow, and then to flame.

But that was all right. That was just as it should have been, really, when you think about it.

And the flames began to dance, as Wonder and Mabel had danced, as Wonder and her mother had danced, and they danced all the way across the floor, where they found Mabel's list turning into ash and nothing, as if it never was. As if it was never the most important thing, after all. Because the list had been the story, for a while, but it wasn't the story any longer.

Now, the story was about Wonder Quinn, only. And what happened to her next, when the candle stopped burning and the attic stopped burning and the lights all went out.

What happened to Wonder Quinn, then?

30
The end

Wonder Quinn sat on the roof of Direleafe Hall. She looked up, towards the stars, to see a familiar shape floating down towards her.

'Hello, Hollowbeak,' she said.

She ran her hand along the shiny new roof tiles. She missed the old shingles. But the fire had eaten them. She supposed, in a way, it was right. It made sense. A new roof for a new year and a new life, without Mabel.

Do you wish you'd never met her? asked

Hollowbeak. *Because I warned you. I warned you it would hurt.*

'How did you know?' asked Wonder.

Because she saw you. None of the others saw you. She saw you because she was like you, in a way. Or very nearly. She was close to becoming what you are.

Wonder leaned her chin on her knees. 'It does hurt,' she said. 'But it is a good sort of hurting. It set me free. I always wondered why I was here and my mother was not. It's because I was weighed down. I wish Mabel never died. But I'm not sad that I cried. It broke me, but it broke the strings, too. The ones that held me here. Is that strange?'

Hollowbeak shook his head. He hopped onto Wonder's knee. She stroked his feathers.

Would you do it again? he asked.

Wonder looked below her. She watched as students tumbled out of the high iron gates, like a school of blue-and-grey-scaled fish, made shining by the sea, swimming away from the mouth of a whale. From where she sat, it was tricky to see who was who.

And, of course, some of them she wouldn't know. There would be newlings in first form.

There might even be another one as magical as Mabel.

But it wasn't that girl she was looking for. It wasn't a student at all.

'No,' she said. 'I only want her.'

She closed her eyes and began to hum.

'My small, precious hatchling,
In your nest, tucked in tight,
Flutter down your eyelids
And bid the stars goodnight ...'

Down from the stars, the music drifted. Another one humming. Another voice. Wonder remembered it.

She looked up at the stars. She knew it was where she came from and where she belonged.

'I could fly,' she said. 'All the way up there. I could.'

Hollowbeak gave a small, sharp nod. *You could*, was all he said.

'Is my mother up there?' asked Wonder. 'Is Mabel?'

Hollowbeak didn't reply for a very long time. Finally, he said, *Perhaps*.

Wonder looked down again. At the girls. At life. It was so noisy and chaotic and beautiful. But it didn't sing to her like the stars did.

'I could fly all the way up there and they wouldn't be there,' she murmured.

'What if they are somewhere else? Somewhere that people go, when they leave straight away? What if I go somewhere different, because it took me longer? I'm afraid, Hollowbeak.'

Hollowbeak leaned his head on her chest. *So am I. But I'll go if you will.*

'I always wanted to go across the seas,' Wonder said, idly. 'To a far-off distant land. I wonder if the stars are like a distant land. Like Abyssinia or Prussia or Siam. I wonder if the stars are like the whole universe, and you can travel through it in the blink of an eye.'

Yes, said Hollowbeak. He seemed to smile. *I imagine that's how they are. I imagine you're free as a bird.*

'She'll be there somewhere,' said Wonder. 'I'll find where she's gone to. And we can be properly friends. Forever.

And I will find my mother, too. And we will be a family and nothing will ever break us and my heart will never break again. Or maybe it will break a million times, but it won't matter. All that will matter is that I have them and they have me and I won't be alone. All of us, Hollowbeak. Together.'

She looked at her bird friend. The one who had been there all along.

'You too, Hollowbeak. All of us together.'

Well, said Hollowbeak, softly. *That would be a thing.*

And then they sat together in silence, watching down below as all the small living things kept on dancing.

And above them the stars danced, too.

And Wonder Quinn and Hollowbeak opened their wings. And flew up. To the stars. To a far-off distant land. Which was a bit like Abyssinia, a bit like Prussia and a bit like Siam.

And nothing like anything you could possibly imagine.

Epilogue

The firemen who came to put out the fire in the old archives room told Ms Gallow that a candle had caused it. And she couldn't believe them because nobody had been up there for years.

She couldn't explain the charred books they found, scattered on the floor.

But she was glad that the old filing cabinet was made from steel and that the records inside it were saved. There was a new cabinet in her office, of course, with the files inside of every student who had lived at Direleafe Hall these past fifty years.

But this old cabinet had been forgotten. Because the stories in the new cabinet were now, and they were happening, and all the stories in the old cabinet were long ago and dust-covered and unimportant.

But as Ms Gallow looked at the old cabinet, she couldn't help thinking about the howling she had heard, the night when Mabel Clattersham died.

And suddenly she knew, it hadn't been Mabel howling.

And there was something else.

Sometimes – just sometimes – when she was in the library alone at night, she could almost swear she heard pages turning. And – only once or twice – when she had gone to tidy her classroom, after the girls had left, she noticed that the chair behind the empty desk was slightly askew. And there was just a ... *feeling* in the air. A smell that felt like memory. As if the room was remembering.

As if someone had *been* there.

And Ms Gallow had a strange sense, now, that perhaps the stories in this cabinet were not long ago and unimportant. Not at all. She had a feeling – in the corner of her brain or in the hairs on the back of her neck – that these stories were *now.*

They were *happening.*

And they were important.

This cabinet was still important.

It contained the files of every girl who had lived at Direleafe Hall in the fifty years before the new cabinets were bought. It told how they lived. It told their stories. For one or two children, it even told how they died.

The first file Ms Gallow came to had a stamp on it that told her that the girl had died while she lived at Direleafe Hall.

She died in a fire, just like the one that had eaten the archives room.

A candle, tipped over. So much golden light, burning everything. Eating everything.

So much light that led to so much darkness.

And to the death of a small girl called Wonder.

But that was less important than all that had come before. The life was what was important. The life was what was golden.

'Wonder Quinn,' Ms Gallow mouthed. 'Let's see how you lived.'

And she read all about the life of Wonder Quinn, who was the daughter of a teacher called Constance Quinn. She read about the bright-eyed, dimple-cheeked girl and her beautiful mother and how they were both so clever and how they both loved each other to the moon ... to the stars.

And, when she was finished, Ms Gallow did not file the story away. She put it beside her, and she retrieved the next story and the next. And she read them all, and then she added them to the pile.

And the pile grew, higher and higher.

So many stories.

And she did not know what she would do with the stories, with the growing pile. She only knew that they would not be locked away, ever again.

And around her there gathered the shadows of all the girls whose stories she read.

And they watched, as Ms Gallow kept reading, on and on, until nightfall.

They watched as she lit a candle, and she read some more.

And outside the window, the silver birch tree swayed in the wind, and the rain fell on the roof of Direleafe Hall.

Acknowledgements

It's a cliché because it's true – no book is created by one person only. Wonder had Mabel and Hollowbeak. I had a whole team of people around me, making this book possible.

Firstly, to Brian, my actual superhero of an agent, who puts up with my neurosis with so much kindness and patience. I don't have adequate words for how irreplaceable he is.

To Kristina, who noticed *Wonder* and championed her. I am so lucky to have had her on my side from the beginning.

To Cathy and Clair, who have been my

cheer squad, wise sages, smile-makers and solvers of all problems. I told them early on that it had been a dream since I was a teenager to be published by UQP. They have made that dream come true and more.

To Kristy, for her astonishingly insightful editing. I felt like she knew and understood Wonder almost better than I did. This book is half hers.

To Rachel, for her incredible illustrations. I've been a fan of Rachel's for years and was beyond excited to hear she would be illustrating *Wonder Quinn*. I am still pinching myself.

Finally, and most importantly, to my family. My dad, Steve, who is my constant source of reinforcement, support, kindness and a soft place to fall whenever I need one. His Leigh, who makes me laugh at the right moment, always. And, most importantly, my Leigh, for his eternal patience and support. And my little Tiger, who inspires me every single day with her bravery, wisdom, vibrancy and wicked humour. I would fly to the moon for you, kid. I would fly to the stars.

Thank you to everyone who reads *The Heartsong of Wonder Quinn*; to everyone who sees her.

I hope you all love it. That would be a thing.

Kate Gordon grew up in a very bookish house, in a small town by the sea in Tasmania. After studying performing arts and realising she was a terrible actor, Kate decided to become a librarian. She never stopped writing and, in 2009, she won a Varuna fellowship.

Kate's first book, *Three Things About Daisy Blue,* was published in 2010. Since then she has written a number of books. Her most recent publications are the young adult novel *Girl Running, Boy Falling* and the younger reader series *Juno Jones: Word Ninja.*

Kate's next book is *The Ballad of Melodie Rose* and will be published in 2021 with UQP.

First published 2020 by University of Queensland Press
PO Box 6042, St Lucia, Queensland 4067 Australia
Reprinted 2020 (twice)

uqp.com.au
reception@uqp.com.au

Cover design and illustration by Rachel Tribout
Author photograph by Stephen Lovell
Typeset in 14/22 pt Adobe Text Pro by Post Pre-press Group, Brisbane
Printed in Australia by McPherson's Printing Group

Australian Government | Australia Council for the Arts

The University of Queensland Press is assisted by the Australian Government through the Australia Council, its arts funding and advisory body.

A catalogue record for this book is available from the National Library of Australia.

ISBN 978 0 7022 6282 1 (pbk)
ISBN 978 0 7022 6411 5 (epdf)
ISBN 978 0 7022 6412 2 (epub)
ISBN 978 0 7022 6413 9 (kindle)

University of Queensland Press uses papers that are natural, renewable and recyclable products made from wood grown in well-managed forests and other controlled sources. The logging and manufacturing processes conform to the environmental regulations of the country of origin.

FSC www.fsc.org
MIX
Paper from responsible sources
FSC® C001695